"My name is Ffion.
I used to tell terrible fibs."

Hana

Ernie

Ellen

Betty

Owen

Francis

FFion

Bert

FFION, THE FROG WHO COULDN'T TELL THE TRUTH
A RED FOX BOOK 978 1 862 30533 5

First published in Great Britain by Red Fox,
an imprint of Random House Children's Books
A Random House Group Company

This edition published 2008

1 3 5 7 9 10 8 6 4 2

Text © Red Fox 2008
Hana's Helpline © 2006 Calon Limited
Hana's Helpline is a registered trademark of Calon.

Red Fox Books are published by Random House Children's Books,
61–63 Uxbridge Road, London W5 5SA

www.kidsatrandomhouse.co.uk
www.rbooks.co.uk

Addresses for companies within The Random House Group Limited can be found at: www.randomhouse.co.uk/offices.htm

THE RANDOM HOUSE GROUP Limited Reg. No. 954009

A CIP catalogue record for this book is available from the British Library.

Printed in China

FFiON

THE FROG WHO COULDN'T TELL THE TRUTH

CRASH! Ffion fell against Mrs Winger's desk. She knocked a vase that was on the corner to the floor. It smashed into lots of tiny pieces.

"Quick!" said Ffion. "Help me clear this up, and don't say anything to Mrs Winger."

It was reading time. Ffion looked in her bag. She couldn't find her book anywhere.

"Ffion," said Mrs Winger, "don't you have your book?"

"I lent it to Ernie," said Ffion, "and he didn't give it back to me."

"That's not true, you fibbing frog," shouted Ernie.

At dinner that night, Francis thought about Ffion. "Mum," he asked, "what should you do if you knew someone had done something bad and blamed someone else for it?"

"Well . . ." said Hana thoughtfully.

"Maybe I should try and persuade her to own up," said Francis. "Thanks, Mum!"

"Glad to be of help," said Hana, "I think you knew what to do."

Ffion and her dad were looking at the photos on the
school wall. "I won so many prizes for my jumping," said
Ffion's dad. "I know you will too!" Ffion looked doubtful.
Then the school bell rang.

   "Sorry Dad, got to go," she said as she ran to
join Francis.

Francis tried to talk to Ffion. "You probably don't know you're doing it, Ffion, but your fibbing isn't making you any friends."

Ffion put her hands over her ears and tried to walk ahead.

"People would like you much more if you told the truth," said Francis. Ffion wasn't listening.

In the classroom Mrs Winger was looking very angry.
"Someone has broken my favourite vase," she said. "It was a
present from my mother."

Looking across at all the little animals, Mrs Winger said,
"Ffion, do you know anything about this?"

Ffion pointed at Francis. "Yes. It was knocked over by a
clumsy little duck!"

In the playground that lunchtime, every time Ffion tried to join in a game with the other children, they stopped playing.

"Francis! Ernie! Let me join in!" she called.

"No one wants to play with a fibbing frog!" said Francis.

Ffion sat on the wall on her own and started to cry.

Ffion decided to go and see Hana. Maybe she would be able to help her. "I've told lots of fibs and everyone is fed up with it," she said to Hana.

"Have you ever thought it might be better to tell the truth?" asked Hana.

Ffion looked alarmed. "I can't do that! My dad would find out and he'd be so disappointed."

The next day Mrs Winger announced she had a surprise for the class. Ffion's dad was coming in to give them jumping lessons. Ffion was very scared. She didn't want to jump in front of her dad. She called Hana for help.

Hana came straight away. "I think it's time you stopped fibbing and told the truth," she told Ffion.

"I can't, not in front of all these people," cried Ffion.

"Is everyone ready?" asked Mrs Winger. "We'll start with leapfrog. Ffion can go first." The rest of the class got into position.

"Now, everyone," said Mrs Winger. "When you get to the end of the line, you crouch down for the next person to leapfrog over. Off you go!"

Ffion looked worried but when Mrs Winger blew the whistle, she started to jump. CRASH! Ffion jumped but she didn't go high enough and she fell on top of Francis. Everyone fell over. They all turned to stare at Ffion and she started to cry.

"I know. It's true. I can't jump at all. I was fibbing the whole time. I wanted my dad to be proud of me and now he thinks I'm a clumsy little frog."

Mr Hopper put his arm around Ffion. "I still love you even if you can't jump. You're my Ffion and that's good enough for me."

Hana gave Ffion a big smile. "And I think you're very brave. It takes a big frog to admit that she's wrong."

Ffion mended Mrs Winger's vase and stopped telling
fibs about being a good jumper. She didn't tell fibs
about anything else either. She just didn't need to pretend
any more.

Hana's Help Point

Hana's Tips if You Can't Stop Fibbing

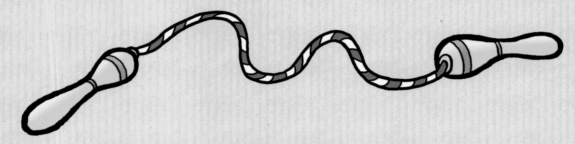

If you tell lots of fibs and can't seem to stop, don't worry! Hana can help!

Why Tell Fibs?

★ Do you want people to notice you?

★ Do you want to believe what you're saying is true?

★ Are you worried that you might upset your parents?

★ Maybe you want to impress friends and be accepted in a group?

★ Are you worried that you'll be told off if you tell the truth?

Help Is Here

★ Once you start telling the truth,
  you'll find that it gets easier and easier.
★ You don't need to tell fibs to make people like you.
★ Remember, it can be harder to tell the
  truth than to lie.

What You Can Do

★ If you have taken something that belongs to
  someone else give it back.
★ If you have broken something try to mend it.
★ It's ok to make up stories as long as you tell people that
  they are made up.
★ Don't fib if you don't like doing something.

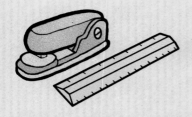

DON'T TELL FIBS!!

"So remember . . .

. . . if you're in trouble and you need help,
ring me, Hana, on **Moo, Baa,
Double Quack, Double Quack!**"